MUCH ADO AT THE ZOO

by Tracey West

Based on
"THE POWERPUFF GIRLS,"
as created by Craig McCracken

SCHOLASTIC INC.

New York   Toronto   London   Auckland   Sydney
Mexico City   New Delhi   Hong Kong

ISBN 0-439-25053-6

Designed by Peter Koblish
Illustrated by Art Ruiz

12 11 10 9 8 7 6 5 4 3 2 1   1 2 3 4 5 6/0

Printed in the U.S.A.

First Scholastic printing, March 2001

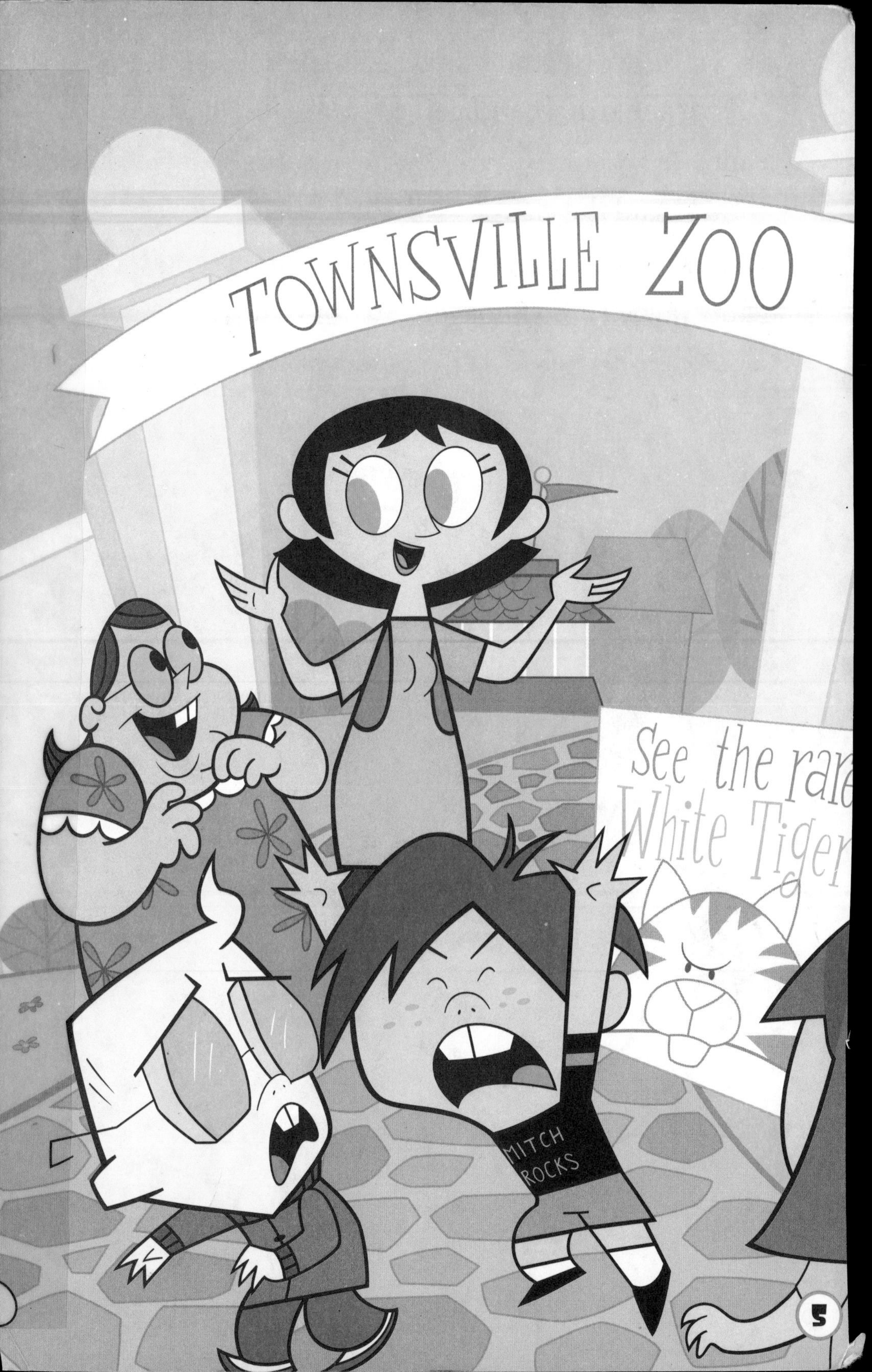
TOWNSVILLE ZOO
See the rare
White Tiger
MITCH ROCKS

"After the trip we will get ice cream," said Ms. Keane.

"Yay!" said the class.

"We will only get ice cream if everyone is good," Ms. Keane warned. "So behave. I do not want any trouble."

The Powerpuff Girls did not want to miss out on ice cream.

"Do not worry, Ms. Keane," said Blossom. "There will be no trouble on this trip. Not as long as we are around."

But trouble was very close.
Mojo Jojo, the evil monkey villain,
was planning something big.

Mojo Jojo surprised The Powerpuff Girls.
"It is I, Mojo Jojo!" he said. "I will steal the rare white tiger. I will spoil your class trip. And you cannot stop me. Ha-ha-ha-ha-ha!"

Buttercup was ready for a fight.
"Come on, Girls! Let's mash that monkey!"
she yelled.

"Wait!" Bubbles cried. "We cannot fight Mojo. If we do, we will not get any ice cream."

"But we cannot let him steal the tiger!" Buttercup said.

"I have an idea," Blossom said. "Bubbles, we need your special power." She whispered the plan to her sisters.

12

Bubbles had a special power. She could talk to animals.

First, she went to the seals.

"Will you help us, seals?" Bubbles asked.

The seals agreed to help. They picked up Mojo Jojo.
They tossed him. They bounced him. Mojo flipped
and flopped in the air.

Buttercup smiled. "Look, Girls. Mojo is having a
ball!"

Mojo landed next to the elephants. "I am dizzy," said Mojo Jojo. "But I, Mojo Jojo, will never give up!"

Next, Bubbles went to the elephants.
"Will you help us, elephants?" asked Bubbles.

The elephants agreed to help. They squirted Mojo Jojo. They sprayed him. They soaked him.

"It looks like Mojo is cleaning up his act!" said Blossom.

Mojo Jojo landed near the penguins.
"I am dizzy. I am wet," said Mojo Jojo. "But I,
Mojo Jojo, will never give up!"

Then, Bubbles went to the penguins.
"Will you help us, penguins?" asked Bubbles.

The penguins agreed to help. They played with Mojo Jojo. They pushed him down the slide. Mojo Jojo splashed into the icy water.

Bubbles giggled. "Look! Mojo is a monkey Popsicle!" she said.

Mojo Jojo landed next to the gorillas.
"I am dizzy. I am wet. I am cold," said Mojo Jojo.
"But I, Mojo Jojo, will never give up!"

The gorillas agreed to help. They hugged Mojo Jojo.
They squeezed him. They tickled him. They would not
let him go.

Ms. Keane and the class saw the gorillas. "Look at the little baby," the teacher said. "Oh, how cute," said the class.

Mojo Jojo could not take it anymore.

"I am not cute. I am not a baby gorilla," he said.

"I am Mojo Jojo. And I GIVE UP!"

The class went to see the rare white tiger.

"It is so pretty," said Bubbles.

"It is so tough!" said Buttercup.

"And now it is safe from Mojo Jojo," added Blossom.

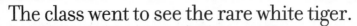

Ms. Keane smiled at the class. "I am so happy there was no trouble on this trip," she said. "Who wants some ice cream?"

"We do! We do!" said The Powerpuff Girls.

So once again, the day was saved, thanks to The Powerpuff Girls . . . and the animals at the zoo!